MW00961676

Diary of a Crafty Adventurer

Book 1: Former or Future Adventurer

Mark Mulle

Copyright © 2016 Mark Mulle

This unofficial Minecraft book is not authorized, endorsed or
sponsored by Microsoft Corp., Mojang AB, Notch Development
AB or any other person or entity owning or controlling the rights
of the Minecraft name, trademark or copyrights. All characters,
names, places and other aspects of the game described herein are
trademarked and owned by their respective owners. Minecraft®/
/TM & ©2009-2016 Mojang/Notch.

All rights reserved.

No part of this publication may be copied, reproduced in any
format, by any means, electronic or otherwise, without prior
consent from the copyright owner and publisher of this book.

Disclaimer
This is a work of fiction. Names, characters, businesses, places,
events and incidents are either the products of the author's
imagination or used in fictitious manner. Any resemblance to
actual persons, living or dead, or actual events is purely
coincidental.

CONTENTS

Diary of a Crafty Adventurer Book 1: Former or Future Adventurer

Day One: My Best Friend

Dear Diary,

My name is Charles, and my life has been pretty crazy recently. A couple of months ago I was on a mission to become a master adventurer, but something--someone-- distracted me. Let me set the scene...

I was just a normal guy from Overworld, but I wanted to be much more. I met this guy who had been known all around the area as the greatest adventurer around...or, he was when he was young. I wanted to learn from this man, and so he sent me on a mission. He sent me to the Nether. I had a great mentor. He used to be a world famous adventurer. He was super famous, but no one knew his real name, so I just called him, "mentor." My mentor had asked me to bring back some Nether wart, the dropped items of defeated monsters, and some other things to prove that I had made it there and out again. This was a challenge for even the most experienced adventurers, so I knew that just making it out alive would be pretty impressive to my mentor. In the end, I did make it out, but not by myself.

While I was in the Nether I met a witch and a blaze who had just snuck out of a Nether prison. At the time, I didn't know what they were in for, I just knew that they needed a way out, and so did I. I helped them to make a portal out of the Nether, but only the witch came out with me. Her name is Verita.

We traveled to Verita's old witch village. We had to go there because I guess things didn't go very well in her last village. There was a problem though, humans like me weren't allowed in the village, and I really wanted to stay with Verita and I am very curious as to how a Witch Village look like. Luckily, she was able to sneak me into the village with the help of an invisibility potion.

While I was in the village, Verita worked on becoming a potion's teacher. She was the best witch at making potions that I've ever seen, so I asked her to teach me how to make potions like her. Over a few weeks, she taught me how to do it. I was even allowed to stay in the witch village once I learned how to make a hard potion, and Verita was allowed to become a real potion's teacher. My life is great right now, but I can't help feeling like I should be doing more...

Day Two: Life in the Witch Village
Dear Diary,

Living in a Witch Village is the weirdest and coolest thing that I have ever done. It almost feels like there is magic in the air. I can buy all sorts of weird stuff here too. A lot of potions need crazy things in them like spider eyes and Nether wart, which are pretty hard to get in most places, but they're just sold here next to melons and eggs. I love the experience of living here, especially since I know that no other human has been able to do it before.

I used to live in a deserted cabin in the woods on the edge of the village when I had to stay hidden--before the witches in the village learned that I knew how to make potions. Part of me wanted to keep living there because I was just so used to it after living there for weeks, but I figured that it was about time that I moved into a real house.

Verita and I rented apartments in the same building. We wanted to live close together, so it worked out well. Our apartments were decorated really differently too. She had posters of different witches on her walls and books scattered all over the place. My house had pictures of explorers, monsters, and weapons lying around.

This morning I woke up in my soft bed and remembered my old life when I had to sleep outside some nights because I was on an important journey. Even though it was hard, I missed that part of my life. I missed my missions, and I even missed my mentor a little bit. I wonder if it would be best if I took on that part of my life again. I think I'll talk to Verita about it tomorrow and see what she thinks.

Day Three: Storytelling and Plain Old Talking

Dear Diary,

I've talked to Verita about my mission before, but I never really went into all that much detail about it. I've told her the basics, like that I was trying to get some materials from the Nether, but I never actually explained why I needed the materials in the first place.

Today I told Verita the whole story. I told her all about my dreams of wanting to be a great adventurer, and how I was on a mission from my mentor, and that's why I was in the Nether. I told her that I got off track of my mission when I met her and her blaze friend. I made sure to mention that I loved spending time with her and living in the Witch Village so that she didn't think that my living her was a waste of my time.

In a way, I was telling this story to prepare her for something that I am going to ask her later. I have been thinking about restarting my mission these last couple of days, and I want to know how she would feel about it, but I don't want to ask her if she would mind if I left if I knew beforehand that she would be crushed if I did. I know that I will miss Verita if I leave, but I guess I want to know how much she would miss me.

I will keep thinking about this for a little while before I ask her anything. This is an important decision, and I want to take my time on it.

Day Four: Witchy Ways

Dear Diary,

I think I figured out why I want to leave the Witch Village and continue working on my goals. Everyone in this village has something to do--something to keep them busy. Even though I am allowed to stay in the village for as long as I want to, no one here wants to hire a human to do work that a witch can do way better. There's not even any monster to hunt around here because the village is so well-protected. As safe and nice as this place is, it's really boring sometimes. A lot of the time, I sit up in my apartment, doing anything but remembering to clean it up, and waiting for Verita to come home from work so that we can hang out.

I know that Verita loves living here, but I don't think that it's for me. Making potions are cool, especially when they explode, and they're even cooler when they do what they are supposed to. Just the other day I figured out how to make an invisibility potion by myself and accidentally scared some kids when I went into town and all they could see was a floating umbrella alone in the rain.

This place comes with its kicks, but I think that tomorrow I will ask Verita what she thinks about my leaving. I'm not going to ask her if it's okay for me to leave though. It's something that I have to do, no matter what. I just hope she takes it well.

Day Five: Finding the Courage to Ask the Question

Dear Diary,

Today is the day that I'm going to ask Verita how she would feel if I left the Witch Village to go back to my training to be an adventurer. So far, she has been at work all day, so I have had a lot of time to think about what I am going to say to her. I figure that I will mention that she spent a lot of time to accomplish her goals to become a potion's teacher, and now I need to spend some time to become the best adventurer that I can be. I hope that this little speech works out because if it doesn't, I have no idea what else I could say to convince her that I had to go if I wanted to be happy. I will continue writing later after I talk to Verita...

I spent the day keeping myself busy. I decided to build a fake enemy out of blocks to pretend to fight. If I was going to go back on my mission I would need to work on my fighting skills. This wooden monster wasn't very hard to fight, so I used a potion to animate the blocks so that it would be able to fight back. While I was in the middle of the fight, Verita came home.

I took out the blockly beat with one final swing of my sword and looked back at her. I asked Verita . "How would you feel if I left to complete my adventurer training?" She told me, "I need to think about it. Can I get back to you tomorrow?" Her voice sounded weird. "Sure," I said.

Day Six: Verita's Answer

Dear Diary,

Verita didn't have to work today, so we had all day to talk, and we did just that.

Verita didn't exactly want me to leave, but she understood that it was something that I had to do. She told me all about her struggles in her old village. All she had wanted back then was to have her own potion's shop. The Villagers in the area didn't like magic, and they made a law against making potions, which was obviously directed at her. She was forced to make potions in secret. She had never told me this whole story before, at least in this much detail, and I guess that selling the illegal potion's was what got her sent to the Nether jail in the first place. Now that she was in the Witch Village, she could finally be herself again. Even though there were a lot of potion's shops in the area and there wasn't much point in opening her own, she was still able to teach, which she ended up loving more than owning her own potion's shop.

After telling me all of this, she told me that she knew that I had to complete my adventurer's training or else I would always be wondering what would have happened if I didn't try, and that was the last thing that she wanted for me. Verita wanted me to be happy, even if it meant not living in the Witch Village anymore. She mentioned that she would be here still if I ever needed her, and I told her that I would make sure to visit.

Tomorrow I am going to start packing for my trip. I hope my training is everything that I remember, and I hope that it'll be worth leaving this great village for.

Day Seven: Planning my Journey

Dear Diary,

Besides leaving Verita, the thing that stinks the worst about leaving is having to pack up and clean out my apartment. Verita stayed with me all day to help me pick up. She looked sad today, probably because she knew that I would be leaving tomorrow. Even though I loved this place, I knew it was time to leave the Witch Village and go back to the human parts of Overworld.

I packed up everything that I thought I would need for my trip. I made sure to stuff my backpack full of anything that might be useful on my trip. I made sure to bring a lot of food since I knew the Witch Village was far from any human or Villager village and I didn't know when I would find a place to get food anytime. Soon. I also brought all of my weapons and tools. I made sure to grab my trusty sword. It wasn't made out of anything fancy like gold or diamonds, but it would get the job done if I ran into any monsters on my way to meet my mentor. I brought a pickaxe and shovel in case I needed to mine anything while I was gone too.

Once I was all packed up, Verita helped me to plan my trip to my old mentor's village. The Witch Village was basically in the middle of nowhere, so Verita made me a map so that I would be able to find my way back to the main roads that would lead me to the other villages. I would need to spend a whole day walking through a creepy forest before I would even have a chance of finding another village. The big forest was one of the ways the Witch Village stayed a secret, so even though it was annoying, I knew it was important. Once out of the forest, I would travel straight to my old mentor's village, then I would begin my training to be the best adventurer ever again!

Day Eight: The Adventure Begins!
Dear Diary,

I left early this morning to begin my adventure to meet my old mentor. I said goodbye to Verita. She gave me a present--a healing potion. She didn't want me to get hurt while I was gone, and even if I did get hurt she wanted me to get better quickly. I thanked her and went on my way.

On my way out of the village, I passed the cottage on the edge of the village that I used to live in before I moved into the apartment building with Verita. Looking at the old cottage brought back memories of what it was like when I first got to the Witch Village.

Part of me didn't want to leave when these thoughts entered my mind, but the rest of me knew that I had to if I ever wanted to be able to complete my goals.

I walked past the cottage and went into the forest right behind it. The forest was just as creepy as Verita said it would be. It was almost like I could feel the magic in the air around me. This forest must be enchanted, I thought while walking. I felt lost while I was traveling in the forest. I wondered if the forest had a spell on it so that humans or other creatures would have a hard time getting to the Witch Village, whether on purpose or accident.

The farther that I got from the Witch Village, the easier it was to stay focused. It was like the forest wanted me to get out of it. Near the end of the day, I could see moonlight peeking out from between the tops of the tall trees around me. I kept walking on, using the moon for guidance.

An hour or two later, I finally made my way out of the forest! I set up a bed by the edge and now I'm going to go to bed. Verita was right, that forest really was something tricky. I wonder if I'll ever be able to find my way back. I hope so.

Day Nine: The Fight

Dear Diary,

I woke up late this morning. I guess that I slept for so long because I spent all day walking through the forest yesterday. It was about noon when I finally got up. I didn't know whether it was time for breakfast or lunch, so I just made a sandwich and called it good. I packed up the rest of my things after eating and starting walking to my mentor's village again.

Now that I was out of the forest it was a lot easier to find my way around Overworld again. I used the map that Verita gave me to find my way around. Luckily, there would be no more forests in my way for the rest of my journey.

I thought today was going to be boring, but something crazy happened while I was walking. I heard a bunch of loud noises while I was walking. At first, I figured that it must be my imagination because I was so tired, but then the noises got louder. They weren't human voices; it sounded more like an animal. I ran towards the noise because it sounded like the animal was in trouble. When I finally found the animal, I also found out that I was right about the noise.

In a clearing, there was a brown horse surrounded by a group of angry-looking creepers. They looked like they were thinking about exploding the horse, but I couldn't let that happen. I put my backpack on the ground and took out my sword. I ran, yelling, to distract the creepers from the horse. I swung my sword at the creepers. At once, they all started looking like they were ready to explode.

I told the horse to follow me as I hid behind a huge pile of rocks. A few seconds later I heard an explosion. I went to look back, and only saw piles of gunpowder on the ground. I collected some of it just in case I would need it. I also decided to take the horse with me, to keep it safe. I gave it the healing potions because the creepers had hurt it. It's nice to have a traveling companion.

Day Ten: The Horse

Dear Diary,

Now that I've got this horse following me around everywhere, I decided to take a detour to a little village on the way to my mentor's village so that I could get a saddle for the horse and some armor for myself in case I met up with any more monsters on my way to my mentor's village.

This was a small village. There couldn't have been more than twenty families living in it. With so little people, I was lucky that there was even someone around who was selling saddles and armor. I guess it was a good thing that this was a farming village. There were so many horses around that I thought I would confuse my horse with some of the other ones around me. That's when I remembered that I actually hadn't named my horse yet.

I thought about naming the horse after Verita, but I thought that it might be weird because we were friends and because I was pretty sure that the horse was a boy. When I met the villager who was selling the saddle I asked him what his name was. He said that his name was Arthur, and that was a good enough name for me, so I decided to give it to the horse.

Once we got the saddle for him, I went to a blacksmith to get some armor. A lot of it was fancy and really expensive, but I didn't have the cash for that. While I did make sure to bring a lot of stuff with me on my journey, I forgot to bring a lot of money. In the end, I had to settle for armor made out of iron ingot; it wasn't flashy, but it would get the job done.

Tomorrow Arthur and I will continue to my mentor's village. We're making some pretty good time, so I think we might actually get there tomorrow.

Day Eleven: My Mentor's Village

Dear Diary,

Putting on the armor and putting the saddle on Arthur made our progress a little slower than it had been yesterday. We had less food because it add on weight, but we also had less food to put into our stomachs, which made us pretty tired for most of the day. I wanted to nap, but I knew that we wouldn't get there any faster by sleeping. I decided to stay up and keep moving even though I was tired. I bet it was nice to be Arthur, getting to eat all of the grass that he wanted and resting whenever he felt like it. I wanted to ask it if it was nice to be a horse, but I obviously couldn't, because you know, he's a horse and can't reply, at least, not in a way that I would be able to understand.

I had a lot of time to think as I travelled to my mentor's village. I wondered if he would still be the same as I remembered him. It had been a few months since I had seen him last. Most importantly, I wondered if he would be upset with me for not completing my mission, or not calling ahead to say that I was coming. Thinking back, I probably should have called so I didn't surprise him. Someone as old as I mentor might not be able to survive a surprise this big. What if my mentor thinks that I'm dead because I never came back from the Nether, well, as far as he knows anyway.

My thinking kept me busy as we kept

moving towards my mentor's old village. When we got there it was already late at night. I decided to stop in a hotel with a barn nearby. I found a nice stable for Arthur to stay the night in, and a room for me to sleep in. I really hope that my mentor will be excited to see me tomorrow. If he doesn't want to take me on again...then I have no idea what I would do next.

Day Twelve: Visiting my Mentor

So, things didn't exactly go as planned today. My mentor doesn't live in the center of his village like a normal person would. He likes his privacy, so he lives near the very edge of the village. Kind of like where I lived when I was hiding out in the Witch Village. My mentor wasn't hiding, though, he was just kind of weird like that. It took me just about an hour to get to his house because I left Arthur in the barn.

I took a deep breath before I knocked on his door. I fixed my hair and made sure to rub out any scuffs in my armor. I wanted to seem professional since this was the first time in a long time that I was meeting up with my mentor. I wanted him to be happy to see me. However, a grumpy old man answered the door. Instead of saying "hi" like a polite person would, he said in a mean tone, "Where have you been?"

Instead of simply talking about my adventures in the Witch Village, I stuttered, "Can I come in?" My mentor nodded and let me in, but he didn't seem happy about it.

Being with my mentor again wasn't very fun. As I had feared, he was extremely upset that I had been gone for so long. He didn't act worried that I hadn't come back, which was pretty offensive by the way, but instead, he just seemed angry that I didn't bring him back any treasures. This didn't match up with his old attitude. He used to be so nice to me. I wondered what had happened while I was gone. I hope he was okay. The best that I had to offer him was the armor on my back, but I didn't think he would be pleased with even that.

All the while that I was there all my mentor wanted to talk about was why it took me so long to get back and why I didn't bring any treasure with me when I didn't come back. I tried to smooth talk my way around his questions because I knew that the Witch Village was a secret, and I didn't want to tell him about it if I didn't have to. However, he eventually kicked me out of his house for not telling. He seemed so weird today. I wonder what was up with him. Even though I don't want to deal with it, I know that I'll have to come back tomorrow and tell him the whole story if I even want him to consider taking me back on as an apprentice. I just hope he'll be a little nicer next time.

Day Thirteen: The Whole Story

Dear Diary,

My visit with my old mentor didn't give me much hope yesterday, to say the least. I really didn't want to go back to his cabin and talk to him again, only to get yelled at for getting off track. I wish I knew someone else who would be able to teach me how to be a great adventure, but finding someone like that would take forever, and I wanted to do this as quickly as possible. So, even though it was the last thing that I wanted to do, I left my hotel this morning and made my way back to my old mentor's house.

It seemed to take forever to get to my mentor's house today, probably because I didn't want to go. It felt just like going to school on my birthday when I was little--it was something I had to do, but something that didn't feel fair either. I knocked on his door again and entered bravely this time, or pretending to be brave, but he didn't know that.

I started talking about my time in the Witch Village right away. I knew if I didn't begin talking about it, then I wouldn't get to it ever. I told my old mentor how I did make it to the Nether, but that I had to help out a witch. I told him how I moved into the village with her and learned all about making potions. I told him that I may have forgotten about my mission for a little while, but that it was all worth it to learn how to make potions and spend a couple of months with Verita. When I was done talking I stood directly across from my mentor and looked at him and waited for him to talk.

Instead of talking right away he led me to the door, pushed me outside, and then closed the door on me without saying a word. I walked back home sadly, wondering where I went wrong. I guess I will just head back to the Witch Village tomorrow. At least, I knew that I had tried to accomplish my goals, but I guess it just wasn't meant to be.

Day Fourteen: Getting a Letter

Dear Diary,

I was all but packed to leave to go back to the Witch Village today. My mentor didn't want to teach me again, and I didn't even know where I would be able to find another mentor. I thought that my whole mission was a waste. As I was heading out the door of my hotel room, I found a letter on the welcome mat outside of my door. I thought about just leaving it there, but something inside of myself told me that I better open it, and boy, am I glad that I did.

I opened the letter and found out that it was from my old mentor. The letter said that he had spent the night thinking about what I had said about the Witch Village, you know, after kicking me out of his house. In the letter, he said that he wasn't sure that he believed that I went to the Witch Village, or that there even was a Witch Village in the first place. The letter ended with my mentor writing, "There are two options for you as far as I am concerned. You can either prove to me that the Witch Village is real and that you were there, or you can get out of town and go back to whatever you were actually doing this whole time."

While it was a little depressing to hear that my mentor didn't believe me, it was understandable. As far as most people knew, the Witch Village was just a myth. It was a story told to Villager kids so that they would stay out of the woods. I knew the truth, though. Now all I would have to do was prove it...and figure out how I'm going to prove it... I'm going to spend the rest of the night trying to figure out what to do, but at least now I know that I still have a chance to complete my goals and become a great adventurer!

Day Fifteen: Sending Letters

Dear Diary,

I have been thinking about it all day, and I think that I've finally figured out how to prove that I was in the Witch Village this whole time. I knew that I couldn't bring my mentor to the Witch Village. Sure, the witches let me inside once, but I doubted that they would let another human into their village if they had the choice. Besides, I'm not so sure that I would be able to find my way through their enchanted forest even if I did have my mentor by my side.

I wrote back to my mentor today to let him know that I wasn't going anywhere. The letter was short and sweet. I didn't want to go into too much detail, so the only thing that the letter said was, "Challenge accepted." After mailing it I realized that I had forgotten to write my name on it, so hopefully he'll be able to figure out who it's from.

I sent another letter today too, but it was too long to fit in this diary entry. For the first time since I've been on my trip, I wrote a letter to Verita. I made sure to tell her everything that I had gone through while I was on my trip. I told her all about making my way through the forest and thanking her for the map that helped me once I got out. I told her about finding Arthur and saving him from the Creepers. Finally, I told her all about the trouble my mentor was putting me through about the Witch Village. At the end of the letter, I asked Verita for a favor. I knew that I couldn't ask for a free pass into the Witch Village, but all that I needed to prove that I was there was a potion, and for that I needed Verita to send me a potion's book. Now all I have to do is wait to get some mail back.

Day Sixteen: Busy Work

Dear Diary,

Even though I don't have the potion's book yet, I know that there are a couple of things that I need to make a potion: a cauldron and a bottle. There's probably some other stuff that's in the potions too, but I was seriously trained for like a month, so I can't remember what they were.

There was one problem with needing to buy things. I don't exactly have...money. Today my hard working skills, cheap manual labor mostly, paid off. There are a lot of old people in this village, and who needs more help than old people? Young people, maybe, but I don't know. I went around town knocking on doors and asking the Villagers who lived there if they needed help with anything. I was so broke that I offered to do anything from washing the dishes to mining for diamonds. Luckily, no one asked me to do either of those things. I spent most of my day walking around collecting blocks for people and making something out of them. I didn't get paid much for my hard work, which is part of the reason why I decided to be an adventurer in the first place, but I did make enough to buy the things that I needed and a little extra too.

I got done working ten minutes before a store closed in town. I rushed inside to buy a cauldron and bottles while I could. The sale's person looked angry that I was in so late, but I couldn't help it. While in the store, I also bought some carrots for Arthur and some cake for me.

I walked back to the stables and had a little picnic with Arthur to share my food. I had a busy day, and I won't be surprised if I fall asleep quickly tonight.

Day Seventeen: Verita's Reply

Dear Diary,

I have no idea what I would have done today if I didn't get a package from Verita. I was glad to see that she sent a potion's book, but I was surprised to see that she had also sent a letter to me too.

The letter that Verita sent me was so long that it might as well have been another potion's book. In her letter, Verita talked about what it was like in the Witch Village without me. Personally, I thought that it sounded boring without me, but Verita was able to keep herself busy.

She said that she had gotten a bunch of new students in the last couple of weeks. Ever since witches in the village had to learn that Verita was able to teach a human how to make potions, all of the witches that had thought that they were too bad at magic to make potions were now coming to her for lessons. I guess the witches figure that if Verita could teach a human, then she would be able to teach anyone. She said that she was having a hard time teaching some witches, but she always loved a challenge and kept doing it. I was proud of her.

Compared to what Verita was up to, my journey sounded really boring so far. I would make up for lost time, though. Once I convinced my mentor that I really had been in the Witch Village while I was gone I was sure that he would give me a super cool mission to prove myself. I was nervous and excited, but mostly I was just ready to do adventure again. I want to be as happy and successful as Verita one day, and that won't happen until I learn to work as hard as she does every day. Even though it might get tough, I know that it will be worth it when I complete my goal.

Day Eighteen: Picking and Posting

Dear Diary,

I missed being in touch with Verita and I missed seeing her every day. I didn't know about any sort of magic that would let me see her again, so I decided to just send her another letter. I wish I could do so much more to show that I still wanted to hang out with her and that I missed her even while I was gone, but I knew that a letter was the best that I could do until I was done with my mission. Once I was a great adventurer like my mentor, I would take a break from all of the treasure seeking, monster hunting, and exploring and visit her in the Witch Village again. Or maybe she could meet me somewhere. I'm sure it would be a lot easier for her to get out of the village than it would be for me to find my way back again.

In my letter, I made sure to thank her, at least, ten times for the potion's book. Looking closer at it, I could tell that it was new, and not one of Verita's old ones. Updated potion's books were expensive, and teachers don't make all that much money, so I was thankful for her gift. I would have to make sure to bring back something nice when I saw her again, but I didn't write that in the letter. If I was going to bring her something I wanted it to be a surprise.

Once I finished writing a letter to Verita I decided to take a closer look inside of the potion's book to pick out what I would make

to prove to my mentor that I really had been

in the Witch Village. I decided to pick

something a little hard to prove that I could

make a potion, but not too hard that I might

mess up and blow my chances of being an

adventuring apprentice again. In the end, I

decided on making a breathing underwater

potion. I figured this would be impressive,

now I just hope that my mentor thinks so too.

Day Nineteen: The Breathing Underwater Potion

Dear Diary,

I only picked the potion I was going to use to prove that I was in the Witch Village this whole time yesterday, so I didn't actually get around to figuring out what I needed to make it. I took another look at the book today to find out. Some of the stuff would be easy to get, but some of it might take some more time. All I needed was water, Nether wart, and a pufferfish. Water would be easy to find around here, and I might need to fish a while to get a pufferfish, but the hardest thing to find around here would be the Nether wart.

Knowing how many potions needed Nether wart, I figured that this must be why more humans don't spend their time making potions. I had no idea where I was going to get the Nether wart from; I was in the middle of Overworld. The last thing I wanted to bother with was going down to the Nether again. That place is creepy, even for me. Anyway, I guess I'll just figure it out when I get to it. I have more important things to do now.

It also turned out that my mentor wasn't happy with the "Challenge accepted" mail that I sent him the other day. He was so upset by it that he actually showed up to my hotel to complain about it instead of just sending another letter. I guess he was mad because he thought that I was trying to disrespect him on purpose. He kept saying stuff like, "I used to be a great adventurer! I deserve more than this!" I guess he had a point. I wasn't trying to be rude to him. I just thought that it would be funny. I was nervous, but I had to explain to him in person why I had picked the Breathing Underwater potion. I told my mentor that it would be really easy to prove that the potion did or didn't work when I was done with it. Either, whatever we used the potion on would live or drown, unless we used it on a fish, which my mentor wasn't going to let me do. I told my mentor that he could watch me make the potion if he wanted, but he said that he trusted me.

Tomorrow I'll begin looking for some of the

supplies for my potion. I hope it goes well.

Day Twenty: Nether Wart

Dear Diary,

The hardest thing on my list for the Breathing Underwater potion was Nether wart, so I figured that it would be a good idea to look for it first so that I would be able to get it over with. I didn't want to bother making a Nether Portal, so I decided to look around the town to see if anyone knew where some Nether wart was or if anyone had some extra that they wouldn't mind giving me.

I spent all day looking for someone who had some Nether wart. I decided to knock on every door in the village to see if someone had any. After ten houses, no one had any.

This village didn't even have a witch in it, which made it all the less likely that there was going to be any Nether wart in this village. None of the people around here looked like they had been to the Nether before, or like they had adventures anywhere for that matter. I knew that my mentor wouldn't have any Nether wart either because that was one of the things he wanted me to get for him while I was in the Nether.

I kept walking around town. It was late when I got to the last house. I thought the Villager inside would have already gone to sleep. I knocked on the door anyway and asked a sleepy Villager about the Nether wart. He said that he did. I asked if I could have it. He said, "You can have it...for a price." I told him that I didn't have much money, and he said that he didn't want money. He wanted me to mine some gold for him because he was too old to do it himself. I agreed.

After a long day of walking around the village, I went back to my hotel room. Now I'm going to collapse on the bed and sleep for a while. I wouldn't be surprised if I kept walking in my dreams.

Day Twenty-One: Gold Miner

Dear Diary,

Even though I was tired last night, I woke up early this morning. I knew that it would take a while to find and mine some gold, and I needed to trade it for the Nether wart as soon as possible. I was glad that I remembered to pack a pickaxe with me before I left the Witch Village. I knew that it would come in handy eventually.

I left my hotel room and went to the stables to find Arthur. I would need to ride him today if I was going to find any gold. I decided to ride far away from the village to find the gold. When Villagers settled in an area they usually took all of the good blocks to make stuff out of it, so there was a small chance that I was going to be able to find any gold there. I decided to ride out to a cave to find the gold. There was always something in a mine that was worth some money, even if I didn't actually find any gold.

I got to a cave about an hour after leaving the village. I decided to make a torch before going inside of the cave. I brought my sword with me too, just in case there were giant spiders inside. I left Arthur outside of the cave so he could eat some grass and nap. I didn't want him getting scared by any monsters that might be in the cave.

I got inside of the cave and started to remove some of the lame rocks that no one would want. I kept digging for hours before I found anything shiny. I found a bunch of silver in the mine, but no gold. Just when I was about to quit I found something great--a diamond!

I left the mine and jumped back on Arthur to ride as fast as I could back to the village. I knocked on the old Villager's door and nearly shoved the diamond in his face. He mumbled something that I couldn't understand, but he still handed me the Nether wart. I brought Arthur back to the stable afterward and took a bath once I got back to my room. Step one of the potion-- done.

Day Twenty-Two: Awkward Potion

Dear Diary,

Every great, or even average, potion maker knows that the base of most potions is the Awkward Potion, and this isn't an exception for the Breathing Underwater Potion that I need to make. There are two basic things that you need to make an Awkward Potion. You need the Nether wart (that I worked so hard to get yesterday) and water (which will be way easier to get today).

I let myself relax for most of the day today since I had worked so hard yesterday. I sold the silver I found in the cave yesterday for some cash. I used the money to buy some treats for Arthur and me, and to pay my hotel bill...which I may have been putting off for a while.

After visiting Arthur with the treats, I decided to find a bucket and fill it with water for the Awkward Potion. I went to a large lake to do this. I stayed there for a while because it was nice out. I felt like going for a swim, but even from the shore, I could tell that there were all kinds of dangerous fish inside. At least now I knew where to come when I had to catch a pufferfish for the potion.

I brought the bucket of water back from the lake and took it to my hotel room. I set up my cauldron and dumped the water inside of it. Next, I needed to add in the Nether wart. I was so excited about getting it yesterday that

I didn't take a good look at it. It was a lot smaller than I had expected, but I guess I deserved it because I didn't actually bring back any gold for the old man. It was a rip-off, though because the old man could buy a bunch of gold with the diamond I bought him. Either way, I threw the Nether wart into the potion. I hope it won't mess it up even if it is small.

I will let the potion brew overnight. Tomorrow I will go fishing to get the last ingredient. Until then, I think I'm going to spend the rest of my day relaxing in the village.

Day Twenty-Three: Fishing Trip

Dear Diary,

There's nothing quite like the open sea, the salty wind on your face and the waves lapping at the side of an old trusty boat, or, at least, that's what fishing books make it sound like. I'm not on a raging sea full of seven-foot tall waves and winds that could blow a mighty ship into the bottom of the ocean; I'm on a small dinky boat that can barely hold me on a little freshwater lake. The waves are hardly a foot high, and the wind smells more like seaweed and fish than salt. As great as they make it sound in books, fishing in real life is pretty boring.

The most annoying part about all of this is that I'm not fishing for fun or food. If that was the case, then I wouldn't be able to catch any kind of fish that I wanted and call it a day. I was fishing for a potion, though, so there was only one kind of fish that mattered to me--a pufferfish. A little fact for all people who have never been fishing before-- fish don't like to be caught, especially not pufferfish.

I sat in my little boat all day with no one to talk to. A couple of times a silverfish got caught on my hook and tried to pull me under, but a pufferfish didn't seem to want to swim near me. In the end, I fell asleep for a little bit, only to wake up to something tugging at my line. I pulled up my line quickly so that I wouldn't lose the fish. Lucky me! I had finally caught a pufferfish. I was glad that my day of fishing was finally over. I was sunburnt all over and tired even after my nap.

Tomorrow I will make the potion. I just hope that it turns out as well as I hope it will.

Day Twenty-Four: Breathing Underwater Potion

Dear Diary,

Today is the day. I finally have all of the supplies to make my Breathing Underwater Potion. All I have to do now is toss in the pufferfish and I should be good to go. Just one more step and the potion would be complete. In my head, I knew that it was a simple task, but on the other hand...procrastinating sounded a lot better.

I figured that I should probably test the Awkward Potion to make sure that it turned out okay before I did anything else. That made sense, right? At least, that's what I told myself when I took an hour to do this simple task. After making sure three times that I did, in fact, make a perfect Awkward Potion, I had to double and triple-check that I had actually caught a pufferfish yesterday. It looked like a pufferfish, but how could I be sure? While it swam in a little tank that I had set up for it last night, I decided to test to make sure that it was a puffy enough pufferfish to use in the potion. I snuck up on it to scare it so that it would puff out. It did seem rather puffy, but how puffy was puffy enough? I read through a potion's book to try to get a sense of how big a pufferfish was supposed to be. Who knows? Maybe I need to go fishing again. It might take a while to find the perfect fish to make the perfect potion...

After reading all about pufferfish for three hours, I realized that I was being really dumb about all of this. I was just nervous. All I had to do was dunk the pufferfish into the potion. So I did, nervously... I picked up the pufferfish by the tail, closed my eyes, and dropped it into the potion. It fizzled a little bit and turned colors, and then it looked like it was starting to brew properly. I won't know if the potion works until tomorrow, so now all there is to do is wait.

Day Twenty-Five: The Finished Product
Dear Diary,

The potion that I made last night seemed to be complete this morning. I carefully dumped every last drop of potion from the cauldron into a bottle. I did my best not to spill a single drop. I wanted the potion to be perfect, and that couldn't happen if I was missing some of it. Who knows how that could affect how the potion works?

Once I had the potion in the bottle I put it in my backpack and went to the stables to see Arthur. I still had some snacks left over from when I sold the silver from the cave, so we shared some apples together today. After our little snack break, I got on his back and we rode to my mentor's house. Even though I was worried that he wouldn't approve, I wanted to show him that I had finished the potion to prove that I had actually been in the Witch Village this whole time.

I nervously knocked on my door. He opened it for me and actually invited me inside of his home for a while this time. I showed him the potion that I had worked on. He took it in his hands and inspected it like he was a detective looking for fingerprints at the scene of a crime. Once he was done looking at it he made a noise that sounded like "Hmm," and handed the bottle back to me.

When I had the bottle again he looked at me and said, "There is only one way to test if this potion really works. If you want to prove to me that you were in the Witch Village and made this potion we will need to test it on something...or someone. I want you to use it tomorrow to prove that it works. Either it will work, and I will take you on as an apprentice again, or it will fail...and so will your air supply."

He left me with that creepy message as he escorted me outside of his house. I rode back to the stables with my head in a daze. I really hope this potion works tomorrow. Not only does my career depend on it, but now my life does too.

Day Twenty-Six: The Challenge at the Lake

Dear Diary,

I woke up early this morning to get ready for the challenge that my mentor had put in place for me. Or, to put it in a more honest way, I got up early this morning because I didn't spend much time sleeping because I was so nervous about what was going to happen next.

I got to the lake before my mentor did. I wanted to take a walk around the lake. I wondered what my mentor would make me do. A little while later my mentor showed up with a key in his hands. Right when I was asking him what it was for, he threw it into the center of the lake. "Find the key and you'll find out what it opens," he said. At least now I knew what I had to do.

I used the Breathing Underwater Potion and jumped into the lake. At first, it felt like I was drowning, but then the water in my lungs felt just like air. The potion had worked! I swam around the lake until I got to the center. Once there, I let my body sink down to the bottom so that I could walk around and look for the key. The sand was soft and slimy beneath my feet. Strange fish were everywhere, and for a moment, I thought that I even saw a giant squid. I kept walking, keeping my eyes on the lakebed below me. Finally, I saw something shiny. I grabbed the key and kicked up back to the surface of the lake. Just in time too! I could feel the potion starting to wear off. I wondered how long I had been underwater.

I swam back to shore and showed the key to my mentor. He snatched it out of my hands. As he was leaving, he said, "I'll see you tomorrow." I punched a fist into the air, happy that I had finally shown my mentor what I can really do.

Day Twenty-Seven: The Results

Dear Diary,

After my challenge last night, my mentor didn't really talk to me all that much. I wanted to visit him, or follow after him, to find out if he was going to take me on as an apprentice again, but I knew that doing that would just annoy him. I decided that it would be best for everyone if I just went back home after the challenge, which is exactly what I ended up doing yesterday.

Now it's today, though, and I can't stop pacing around my house wondering what will happen next. I can't sleep, I can't eat, I can't do anything until I know if my mentor will take me back on again. I feel useless. Whatever my mentor says today will determine what I do for the rest of my life. Either I can be the world's greatest adventurer to ever live, or I can be some nobody who failed out of adventuring and grew old...never doing more than mining for the rest of his life, and that kind of life just isn't the life for me.

I waited around anxiously for a while now, and I'm starting to lose it. Wait? What was that? I just heard a noise. I'm going to go and check it out.

Diary! The best thing just happened. The noise I heard was a letter being pushed under my door. At first, I thought it was just another letter from Verita, but then I noticed that it was in my mentor's handwriting. I quickly opened the envelope and read the letter. Even though his penmanship would make it seem otherwise, my mentor was going to gladly take me on as a student again since I proved that I had discovered the Witch Village and learned their secret art of making potions. The letter told me to meet him at his house tomorrow for more details, which means that I'll write more here tomorrow to update this diary.

Day Twenty-Eight: Part One of my Mentor's Meeting

Dear Diary,

I guess that my mentor is a busy guy, so he only had a short amount of time to talk to me today. It was actually pretty boring. He was just telling me things that I already knew. Today my mentor wanted to talk about my last mission. Honestly, I think he just likes to rub the fact that I never actually finished. He was asking me all sorts of weird questions about it too. Like, "Do you remember what supplies I told you to get from there?" and "Do you even remember how to make a Nether Portal?" and "Who doesn't know how to make a Nether Portal?" That might have been when I realized that part of the reason my mentor and I were never best friends was because we were so different from each other. He was this old guy who couldn't even go on missions anymore, and I was this young guy who could goes on any mission, anywhere. I think he was jealous of my youth, and I was jealous of his experience.

In the end, the meeting just left me feeling really confused. I'm not really sure what I was even supposed to take away from it. The whole time my mentor was talking about my old mission. I just feel like he was wasting my time today. I already know all about my old mission, I was there. I wanted to hear about the new mission that my mentor was going to put me on, but I guess that telling me about my new mission must be on his to-do list for tomorrow because he scheduled another meeting with me then. I hope that this meeting will be more exciting than the one I just had. Then again, when are meetings ever exciting?

Anyway, I'm going to hang out with Arthur for a little bit, maybe ride around the village. I don't know what I want to do, but I know that I need to do something exciting before I die of boredom.

Day Twenty-Nine: Part Two of my Mentor's Meeting

Dear Diary,

I really didn't feel like going to my mentor's house for another boring meeting today, but I knew that if I ever wanted to be a world-case adventurer I would need to seek my mentor's advice, even when it was less than exciting. I decided to take Arthur with me this time, just in case it got really lame and I needed to do something adventurous right afterward.

I walked into my mentor's house today. For once, I wasn't nervous about what he might say. Since I knew that he was going to teach me how to be an adventurer again, I wasn't as scared around him anymore. Even if he got mad at me, I knew that he wouldn't go back on his word. He just wasn't that kind of guy.

Today my mentor decided to actually talk to me about what my next mission was going to be. He told me that to be a real adventurer I needed to go on, and complete three missions. He figured that my adventure in the Witch Village was good enough to count as one, so now I needed a second mission. I was a little nervous when he said this because the look on his face changed. He looked like he was about to play a mean trick on me, and when he actually told me my new mission I thought he was joking. Sadly, mentors don't joke. He said, "Your new mission will be an old mission. You will go back to the Nether and finish the mission that you got so distracted from last time I sent you on it. You will need to collect the same supplies, fight the same villains, but this time, avoid falling for a witch along the way."

I didn't know what to say. The whole thing just seemed really confusing. All I could think so say was, "Okay."

My mentor led me out of his house. As I looked back, I could see him smile. "You passed the hardest test," he said.

"I know," I replied. "Making that potion took a lot out of me."

"No," he corrected me. "You were able to deal with a rude old man for weeks without snapping at me. Being able to respect your elders is a true sign of a great adventurer. It's nice to know that you can still respect a retired adventurer."

"Of course I respect you," I said. "You were the coolest adventurer back in the day. I used to have posters of you in my bedroom when I was a kid. Everyone wanted to be like you." I thought for a little longer before asking my next question. "So...does this mean that things will go back to normal between us? Are you going to start acting nicer again?"

My mentor chuckled. "Of course. After all, I respect you too, now."

I climbed back on Arthur slowly after our conversation and he brought me back to my hotel. I was so confused. I had to go on my old mission again. I needed to lie down and think about this for a little while.

Day Thirty: What Now?

Dear Diary,

I have my mission. My destiny is staring me in the face. I shouldn't feel like there's a problem. I can't put my finger on it, but I think it might be because I've already been to the Nether. Even though I didn't complete my mission last time I don't think that I should have to do it again. It just seems unimportant. I want to try something new to teach me about being an adventurer, not doing the same thing over and over again.

At least, I know that the Nether is an exciting place to be. I don't know what my adventure is going to be like, but I do know that there's going to be a lot going on. I'll need to start a whole new diary to fit in all of the exciting stuff that I'm doing to do. I hope Arthur will want to come too.

I wonder what sort of crazy stuff will happen in the Nether? I guess I just need to wait to find out!

Made in the USA
Las Vegas, NV
14 December 2020

13352579R00056